Davide Calì & Monica Barengo

The Writer

DAVIDE CALÌ has written over one hundred children's books, which have been published in over thirty countries. His picture books include *Grown-Ups Never Do That* (Chronicle), *I Hate My Cats* (Chronicle), and *The Queen of the Frogs* (Eerdmans). Born in Switzerland, Davide now lives in Italy.

MONICA BARENGO is an Italian artist and illustrator. Her work has been exhibited at the Bologna Children's Book Fair, and she has been twice selected as a finalist by the Golden Pinwheel Young Illustrators Competition in Shanghai. *The Writer* is her first book published in English. Visit her website at monicabarengo.com or follow her on Instagram @monica.barengo.

For Monica
d.c.

First published in the United States in 2022
by Eerdmans Books for Young Readers,
an imprint of Wm. B. Eerdmans Publishing Co.
Grand Rapids, Michigan

www.eerdmans.com/youngreaders

Text © 2019 Davide Calì
Illustrations © 2019 Monica Barengo
Originally published in Italy as *Lo scrittore*
© 2019 Kite Edizioni
www.kiteedizioni.it

English-language translation © Eerdmans Books for Young Readers 2022

Manufactured in the United States of America

30 29 28 27 26 25 24 23 22   1 2 3 4 5 6 7 8 9

ISBN 978-0-8028-5585-5

A catalog record of this book is available from the Library of Congress

Illustrations created with graphite pencil and digital media

Davide Calì & Monica Barengo

The Writer

Eerdmans Books for Young Readers
———————————————
Grand Rapids, Michigan

There he is.

TIC
TI TIC

TIC

TIC
TI TIC TIC
TIC TIC

I get up, and he's already
sitting there with his
tic-tic-tic.

Of course it's irritating.

Some days he doesn't even get dressed.
He just stays there in his pajamas, writing
and drinking coffee.

If it weren't for me,
he wouldn't even
remember to eat.

To be honest, he's never had a very
intelligent look about him.
Sometimes I wonder: what is he thinking?
And most of all: what is he writing?
I suppose this must be his work.

TIC

TI TIC

TIC

Ugh . . .

He writes all the time.

TIC TIC

TI TIC TIC

Luckily I'm here.

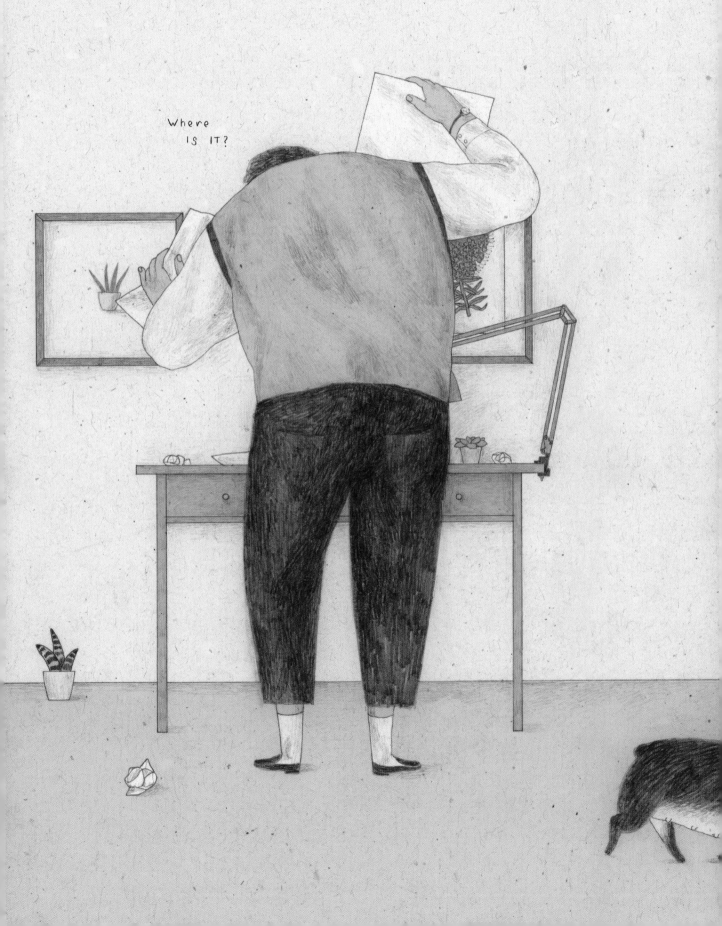

Every now and then he needs
to be distracted.

But I can't do everything myself.
I think he needs someone else.

For example, that person seems quite nice.

But no, he never understands anything.

Where is he looking?

Has he seen that other one over there?

Obviously not.

At this rate, he'll always be on his own.

And this one — what
does she want?

Not this one!

I can't believe it—
are they talking?

No, please,
not this one!

Let me tell you clearly:
we really don't need . . .

. . . another dog!